OLIVIA
Opens a Lemonade Stand

adapted by Kama Einhorn

based on the screenplay by Eryk Casemiro and Kate Boutilier

illustrated by Jared Osterhold

Simon Spotlight

New York   London   Toronto   Sydney

Based on the TV series *OLIVIA™* as seen on Nickelodeon®

SIMON SPOTLIGHT
An imprint of Simon & Schuster Children's Publishing Division
1230 Avenue of the Americas, New York, New York 10020
Copyright © 2010 Silver Lining Productions Limited (a Chorion company).
All rights reserved. OLIVIA™ and © 2010 Ian Falconer. All rights reserved.
All rights reserved, including the right of reproduction in whole or in part in any form
SIMON SPOTLIGHT and colophon are registered trademarks of Simon & Schuster, Inc.
For information about special discounts for bulk purchases, please contact
Simon & Schuster Special Sales at 1-866-506-1949 or business@simonandschuster.com.
Manufactured in the United States of America 0511 LAK
9 10
ISBN 978-1-4169-9932-4

It was a hot summer day, and Olivia was busy opening up her very own lemonade stand. Ian and Julian helped make the lemonade. They squeezed lemon juice into a pitcher of water, added sugar, and stirred.

"Fresh-squeezed lemonade," Olivia said. "Everyone's going to want to buy some of this. I've dreamed of opening a lemonade stand my whole life!"

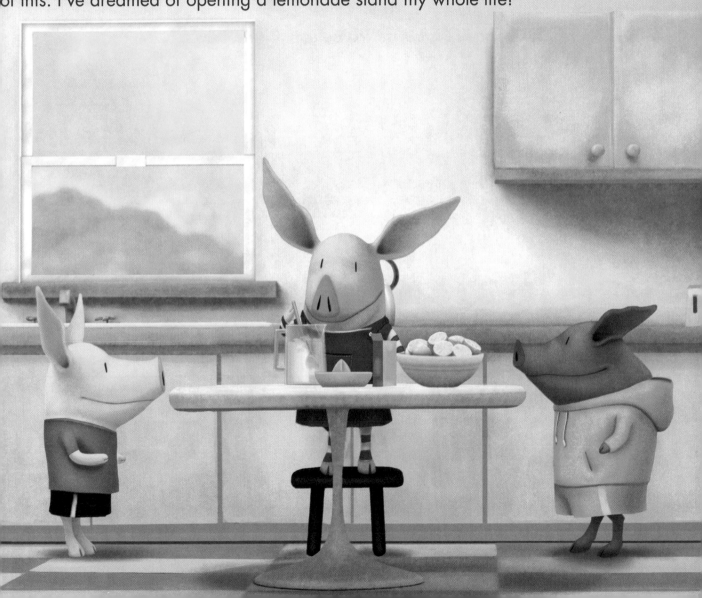

"Olivia's Lemony Lemonade stand is open for business!" declared Olivia. She poured a cup for Julian. "Now I need you to be totally honest," she said. "Isn't it delicious?"

"S . . . s . . . sour!" gasped Julian.

"Well, lemonade is *supposed* to be sour," said Olivia.

Then Olivia tried the lemonade herself. Ack! "Okay, it's a little sour," she admitted. "I'd better fix this before customers get here. Ian, go fill this cup with sugar and bring it back."

"Say please," said Ian.

"Please," said Olivia. "Now *please* hurry!"

Ian went to the kitchen and called out to his mother.
"Where's the sugar?" he asked.
"In the cabinet, next to the salt," she answered.

Ian rushed the cup back to Olivia, who added it to the lemonade just in time to say, "Good morning, Mrs. Hoggenmuller! Would you like a cup of my Lemony Lemonade?"

"Yes, please," said Mrs. Hoggenmuller. "Oh, there's nothing more delightful than a delicious glass of lemonade on a hot summer's day. In fact, I'll take two."

"What do you think?" asked Olivia.

"Mmmm-gggg-phhhhh . . . too . . . salty!" cried Mrs. Hoggenmuller.
"Wow, look at her face!" said Harold, who had stopped by with Daisy.

"Is your lemonade sour? We love anything super-sour," said Daisy.
"Yep. That's why I call it Olivia's Super-Sour Lemonade! You've come to the right place!" said Olivia.
They both took a sip. "Ugh! Salty!" said Harold.
"It tastes like the ocean," said Daisy.

"Ian! You gave me salt, not sugar!" Olivia cried.

"Oops!" Ian said. "Sorry, they're both white."

"This is my Super-Sour-Kind-of-Salty one, but I have two other pitchers of Super-Sour Lemonade coming right up," Olivia assured her customers.

Then Olivia saw Francine next door in her driveway, calling out "Fresh strawberry lemonade! Get your strawberry lemonade here! It's pink and yummy—and *unsalted*!"

When Francine noticed Olivia, she said, "Oh, hello there, Olivia. Would you like some strawberry lemonade?"

"No thank you," said Olivia. "I have my *own* lemonade stand."

"I'll be right back with more paper cups, everybody," said Francine proudly. "I had no idea it would be such a hit!"

Now Francine had lots of customers, and Olivia had none. "I don't want a lemonade stand anymore anyway," Olivia told Julian.
"But, Olivia—you've wanted one your whole life!" said Julian.
"I mean . . . I don't want *just* a lemonade stand anymore," she said. I wonder what it would be like to have my very own restaurant . . . , Olivia thought.

It's Olivia's . . . Olivia's Restaurant! Thanks for coming,
it sure does mean a lot.
Welcome to Olivia's, where the food is delicious and
everything is served with Super-Sour Lemonade!

"We've got work to do . . . in my *new restaurant*!" Olivia told her staff. "Come on!"

"If I'm cooking and Julian's walking around with a towel on his arm, what are you doing?" Ian asked Olivia.

"It's my restaurant," explained Olivia patiently. "My job is to walk around and sing and make sure people are having fun. Oh—customers!" she cried. "Ian, start cooking. Julian, start doing waiter stuff."

"Good afternoon, Daisy. Hello, Harold. Welcome to Olivia's Restaurant," said Olivia.

"The cracker and banana appetizer is very good tonight. Your waiter will be right with you. To start, here are two cups of Olivia's Super-Sour Salt-Free Lemonade."

"Mmm, really sour," said Daisy.

"I can hardly move my tongue," said Harold happily.

"I'm supposed to tell you that this is today's special: Fruity cereal nuggets with gravy," Julian said. "I'll be right back with the main course . . . uh, spaghetti and raisins."

"This is the best restaurant ever!" said Daisy.

Oscar and Otto came by too. "Hi, Oscar. Hi, Otto. I hope this table is okay," Olivia said.

She noticed an angry squirrel was in the tree above, dropping acorns on her customers. But Oscar and Otto didn't mind.

"Oh no, we like it," said Oscar.

"It's cool," said Otto.

Ian stayed busy cooking in the kitchen. "Look, Mom,
I'm a chef!" he said proudly.

Sophie and Caitlin came by next.

"Excuse me. Do you have any sour pink grapefruit jelly beans?" Sophie asked.

"How about pink marshmallow watermelon kebobs?" asked Caitlin.

"They only eat or drink pink food," Julian explained to Olivia.

"Pink food?" said Olivia. "That's the one thing we don't have!"

Olivia knew just what to do. She went straight to Francine. "Two glasses of your strawberry lemonade, please," she said. "It's for some customers at my restaurant. Francine poured the glasses and also gave Olivia some for herself. "This is really good, Francine," Olivia told her.

"Thank you," said Francine. "But running a lemonade stand isn't as much fun as I thought."

"Having a restaurant is lots more fun," said Olivia.

"If you're tired of the same old juice box, then come to Olivia's restaurant, home of Francine's Strawberry Lemonade," Olivia announced. Then she looked at her band. "Hit it!" she said.

"We're Olivia's—and Francine's Pink Strawberry Lemonade! Oh, yeah!"

And so Olivia and Francine became partners. Running a restaurant was hard work, but it was really fun when everyone did it together.

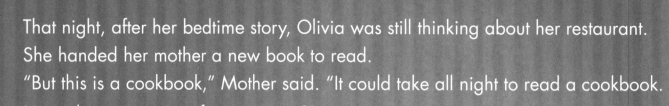

That night, after her bedtime story, Olivia was still thinking about her restaurant.
She handed her mother a new book to read.
"But this is a cookbook," Mother said. "It could take all night to read a cookbook.
How about we save it for tomorrow?"

"Well . . . all right," agreed Olivia. "Good night, Mom.
"Good night, sweetie."